It's ALL ABOUT ME!

By Nancy Cote

G. P. Putnam's Sons   New York

G. P. PUTNAM'S SONS
A division of Penguin Young Readers Group
Published by The Penguin Group
Penguin Group (USA) Inc., 375 Hudson Street, New York, NY 10014, U.S.A.
Penguin Group (Canada), 10 Alcorn Avenue, Toronto, Ontario, Canada M4V 3B2 (a division of Pearson Penguin Canada Inc.)
Penguin Books Ltd, 80 Strand, London WC2R 0RL, England.
Penguin Ireland, 25 St. Stephen's Green, Dublin 2, Ireland (a division of Penguin Books Ltd.)
Penguin Group (Australia), 250 Camberwell Road, Camberwell, Victoria 3124, Australia (a division of Pearson Australia Group Pty Ltd).
Penguin Books India Pvt Ltd, 11 Community Centre, Panchsheel Park, New Delhi - 110 017, India.
Penguin Group (NZ), Cnr Airborne and Rosedale Roads, Albany, Auckland 1310, New Zealand (a division of Pearson New Zealand Ltd).
Penguin Books (South Africa) (Pty) Ltd, 24 Sturdee Avenue, Rosebank, Johannesburg 2196, South Africa.
Penguin Books Ltd, Registered Offices: 80 Strand, London WC2R 0RL, England.

Published simultaneously in Canada. Manufactured in China by South China Printing Co. Ltd.
Design by Katrina Damkoehler. Text set in Berliner Grotesk Light.
The art was done in gouache and watercolor pencil on Arches paper.

Library of Congress Cataloging-in-Publication Data
Cote, Nancy. It's all about me / by Nancy Cote.   p. cm.
Summary: A little boy is upset and jealous when his baby brother is born, but his parents reassure him
that he is still special.   [1. Babies—Fiction. 2. Brothers—Fiction. 3. Jealousy—Fiction.
4. Stories in rhyme.] I. Title: It is all about me. II. Title.
PZ8.3.C82836It 2005   [E]—dc22   2004024736

ISBN 0-399-24280-5

1 3 5 7 9 10 8 6 4 2

First Impression

To my godchildren: Suzy, Kevin,
Andrew, Ariel, and Cody

I cry

I sleep

I kick my feet

I even suck my toes

I laugh

I crawl

I roll around

I also pick my nose

And Mommy tells me I'm the best
And Daddy tells me, too
    And when I smile they say I'm great
    No matter what I do

I sit

I walk

I try to talk

I push my bike on wheels

I feed myself

I play in mud

I love how squishy it feels

And Mommy tells me I'm the best
And Daddy tells me, too
And they will always love me
That I know is true

I run

I play

I hear them say
A baby brother is on the way
I don't want a baby boy
I'd rather have a brand-new toy

If Mommy tells me I'm the best
And Daddy tells me, too
    Then why'd they want another one?
    Oh, I hope that it's not true

I watch   I see

He looks at me

I look at him, too

He screams

He bangs

He spits

And laughs

His hair gets stiff like glue

When Mommy says he looks so cute
I don't know what she sees
    I hope that baby disappears
    And then she'll just have me

I cry

I'm sad

I get so mad
I wish he'd go away

He drools

He smells

He smiles at me . . .
Well, maybe he can stay

I am the older brother
And the baby is brand-new
My little baby brother
A monster dressed in blue

I write   I read

Sometimes I need
A quiet place to play

My brother follows me around
He does this every day

And Mommy tells me I'm the best
Big brother that she knows

Someday we'll play together
I can't wait until he grows

I hear

I see

A baby three
Is coming home today

My brother won't be happy
He'll want to run away

But I tell him a family's best
Our parents tell him, too

So welcome, little baby

Little baby, we love you!